DATE DUE

FE 10 '92	21		
JA 18 '93	6		
FE 07 '93	9 9		
JA 15 '96	16		
FE 24 '96	3		
OCT 11	4		

HOORAY for Father's Day!

by Marjorie Weinman Sharmat

illustrated by John Wallner

Holiday House/New York

Printed in the United States of America

Library of Congress Cataloging-in-Publication Data

Sharmat, Marjorie Weinman.
Hooray for Father's Day!

SUMMARY: Father Mule's two loving children spend Father's Day showering him with lively presents that leave him exhausted, when the gift he really needs is a dose of peace and quiet.
[1. Mules—Fiction. 2. Father's Day—Fiction. 3. Gifts—Fiction. 4. Fathers—Fiction] I. Wallner, John C., ill. II. Title.
PZ7.S5299Hm 1987 [E] 86-15037
ISBN 0-8234-0637-7

For my wonderful dad,
NATHAN WEINMAN,
and the annual search
for his perfect present
M.W.S.

For Sal
J.C.W.

Father Mule lived with his two children, Sterling and Monica, in a small house in a big canyon.

Once a year, on Father's Day, Sterling and Monica did a lot of extra things for their father. But this Father's Day was going to be the best yet.

"I am going to do all kinds of wonderful things for Father," Sterling said.

"I am going to buy Father some wonderful presents," Monica said.

"It's better to *do*," Sterling said.

"It's better to *buy*," Monica said.

On Father's Day Sterling said to his father, "You should be able to be lazy all day long and not lift a hoof to do anything. I am going to make you a great Father's Day breakfast. What would you like?"

"How about a toasted muffin with a dash of cream cheese and a small glass of milk?" his father asked.

"Coming up," said Sterling.

He toasted ten muffins, spread cream cheese over them, put them on a tray and took them to his father along with five quarts of milk.

Sterling's father struggled to eat his breakfast. Then he lay down on the sofa. "I think I ate too much," he said. "But I do appreciate all the muffins and cream cheese and milk. Your efforts are extraordinary, Sterling."

"So are mine," Monica said. "I saved up my allowance for fifty-two weeks and I bought you a jump rope and a sweatband so you can exercise."

"Exercise?" said Father Mule. "I just ate. I can't exercise right after eating. I will exercise tomorrow."

"But tomorrow isn't Father's Day," said Monica.

"Right, right," sighed Father Mule.

"Let's go outside," said Monica, "and you can jump there."

Father Mule and Sterling and Monica went outside. "Now jump, Father," Monica said.

Father Mule jumped and jumped and jumped.

"I feel silly," he said. "And I feel tired. But these are lovely presents. A jump rope and a sweatband are two things I will look at with great pleasure."

"Look at?" said Monica.

"What Father means is that he's tired from jumping and needs a bath," Sterling said. "That is where my present of *doing* things comes in. How about a nice bath, Father, with a little army of rubber ducks in the water to keep you company, and I'll sprinkle you all over with cornstarch afterwards."

"Ducks? Cornstarch?" said Father.

"I knew you'd be happy about that," Sterling said as he dragged his father back into the house.

"Into the bathtub!" Sterling said. "And you can splash all you want with your duckies."

When Father Mule was finished with his bath, Sterling dumped cornstarch all over him. "You're the cleanest father in the canyon," Sterling said.

"Ducks and cornstarch for Father's Day!" Monica said. "That *won't* do it. What Father needs is a picnic! I bought tickets to the Annual Mule Picnic and Band Concert. I even bought a ticket for you, Sterling, so you wouldn't feel left out."

"I do like picnics," Father Mule said.

"Then follow me," said Monica.

Up and down the canyons Monica led the way. She led Father Mule and Sterling into the picnic grounds.

Father Mule looked around. "There must be two thousand mules here!" he gasped.

"Yes, isn't that great!" said Monica. "You should not feel lonesome on Father's Day."

Father Mule, Monica, and Sterling lined up for their food. It was a long line and they stood for a long time.

"I wonder if Father's Day is over yet," said Father Mule. "We've been waiting so long it's beginning to feel like tomorrow has come."

Finally their turn came. Father Mule, Monica, and Sterling piled food on their plates. Then they sat down under a tree.

"Oh look!" said Monica. "Here comes the Mule Marching Band. The music's starting!"

Father Mule covered his ears.

After awhile Sterling covered his ears.

Then Monica covered her ears.

“I can make better music for you at home, Father,” Sterling said, “by banging together a washtub and several pots and pans. I will do that for you when we get home.”

“Let's just leave,” said Father Mule.

Father Mule, Monica, and Sterling staggered out of the picnic grounds. They were still holding their ears.

They started to walk home.

Suddenly, Father Mule stumbled.

"Oo-oo-oo-ops!" he cried as he slid into a canyon.

Monica and Sterling slid down behind him. They all landed in a heap.

"What a disgusting thing to happen on Father's Day," said Monica. "This wasn't in my plan."

"It wasn't in mine, either," said Sterling.

Slowly, hanging on to each other, Father Mule, Sterling, and Monica pulled themselves up out of the canyon.

They straggled home under the stars.

They all collapsed in chairs.

"Now don't you worry, Father," Sterling said, looking at his watch. "Father's Day isn't over yet. There are other things I can do for you."

"Just a minute," said Monica. "I have other things I've bought for you."

Father waved his arms. "No, no, no! I have had muffins and milk and a jump rope and sweatband and duckies and cornstarch and a picnic with blasts of music, and even a fall down a canyon that wasn't meant to be a present. Now I want peace! I want quiet!"

"I can't do peace," said Sterling.
"I can't buy quiet," said Monica.

"I'll settle for a barbecue," said Father Mule, "with my kids under the quiet stars."

And that's what they had.

"No more presents!" said Sterling. "Hooray!"

"No more presents!" said Monica. "Hooray!"

"Hooray for Father's Day and my two wonderful children!" said Father Mule.